The Wife Who Wanted to Dance

A K Hazelton

The Wife Who Wanted to Dance
First published 2020 by Compass-Publishing

ISBN 978-1-913713-24-9

Typeset by The Book Refinery Ltd
Cover design by A K Hazelton

Dedication

To all the people who inspired me to write this story!

Peter's Story

'So, would you go dancing, then?' Geoff asked.

'Don't even go there, mate,' I replied, taking hold of my pint and enjoying a long swig.

It was nearing the end of a typical Saturday night at the pub. Most of the lads had drifted away after we'd all put the world to rights. Geoff and I had been left finishing our drinks, when he decided to have a moan about his wife – or, as he called her, 'the old trout'.

'I've had it up to here, mate,' he said, 'and the final straw is, she wants us to go dancing!'

I laughed without this being funny. Poor sod, I thought.

It was then he put me on the spot. He didn't bother looking for an explanation from me: my tone of voice and body language must have said it all.

I could, however, have told him of my experience last year...

***

Slumped unhappily on the plastic chair, I glanced up as the lady dance coach walked towards me, with an annoying grin.

As if things weren't bad enough, this was now pushing the whole miserable experience to new heights. How had things come to this?

To understand how this ordeal at a modern jive dance class had started, we need to go back to a day a few weeks before this where it all began.

I'd woken that morning to the realisation that the alarm had not gone off. Of course, it was Saturday and the weekend lay ahead. But first, some extra time in bed. I sensed my wife, Shirley, was already awake so I turned and snuggled up. Happy days! I then thought about the possibility of taking things further and starting the day with a bit of morning delight.

I began the charm process: 'Shirl… how about some fun to start the day?'

'Not now, I'm resting,' came the dreary reply.

Worth a try, I thought. But there was always tomorrow.

As she started to snooze, I spent a few moments going through the forthcoming day in my head. After a busy week in my job as a kitchen and bathroom fitter, I was now going to have some me-time. A morning in the man shed, pottering about; maybe repairing that chair I kept promising to fix, and, of course, listening to the sport on the radio. A quick bit of lunch and then off to football. The Blues were at home so it would be a few beers with the lads and then on to the game – the bonus being I'd heard Shirley chatting all week on the phone to friends and family about *Strictly Come Dancing*, which was starting again on the box that weekend, so that would mean I could stay in the pub afterwards without being missed. Dinner would be in the microwave later in the evening and the job was done. Deep joy.

With this sorted in my head, I decided to treat myself to another ten minutes in bed. Good decision, I thought, as I heard raised voices. Already the fighting for the bathroom had begun.

We had two daughters, Amy (19) and Caroline (21), both of them still living at home. If the last few years were anything to go by, then from September through to Christmas on a Saturday night, I would see the pair of them with Shirley transfixed in front of the box. Both girls had boyfriends, but they'd learnt to keep clear on Saturday evenings or, if they did stop by, to be quiet. If a snarky comment left their lips, fallout would usually take place. Those boys learnt quickly it wasn't worth it. Anyway, this reprieve allowed me to go to the pub with the lads and I looked forward to that weekly evening out.

It was when we got down to breakfast that things took an unexpected turn. I hadn't noticed the weather yet but, when I did look outside, I could see it was raining heavily. Innocent enough, except that Shirley had planned a morning in town for a coffee and catch-up with her best friend, Pat, who had called to cancel. She had to take one of her kids to their morning activity due to the rain. Pat was single and was often the taxi for her kids. Her husband had died a few years back and, as they'd waited a little longer to have their second child, poor Pat was often pulled from pillar to post juggling her job and bringing up her young son and teenage daughter.

The consequence of this cancellation was Shirley deciding this would be a great opportunity to take me along to help with and sample the delights of… the weekly food shop. This was a job she would normally have done on Friday on her way home from work. She worked part-time at a hairdressing salon but this week had arranged to stay and have her hair done after her shift finished.

Food shopping – annoying, but why not? It would get me brownie points with her, and football beckoned afterwards along with those beers with the lads. Win some, lose some.

The journey to the local superstore was uneventful enough, my head full of the forthcoming football later that afternoon, while Shirley chatted on excitedly about the dancing programme that evening. How sad, I thought, but if it keeps her happy…

The car park was busy but I still managed to get a spot close to the store. Shirley had gone strangely quiet, as she often did, and we joined the queue, walking slowly towards the escalator.

We were about halfway up when I became aware of music. Shirley seemed to perk up and started to tap her foot and hum along. I remember thinking it was a song from that film, *Dirty Dancing*, and I only knew that because she must have watched it a thousand times over the years, often with the girls.

We reached the top of the escalator. What greeted us was the sight of about a dozen couples dancing to the music, smiles on their faces, most of them in brightly coloured T-shirts with the name of a dance group on them. Almost stopping our progress into the store was a big pop-up banner with the same logo and name written on it. My eyes caught the message: 'Modern jive dancing. Come along to classes at the local hall. No partner needed. Make new friends. Great for health and fitness.'

I quickly read these words and told myself this might as well be a promotion for Marmite, such was my dislike of both things.

But I was then distracted by several alarming factors that seemed to be happening completely out of my control.

Shirley had, since halfway up the escalator, been jigging around, humming along with the song. Upon reaching the top, her face broke out into the hugest smile I could remember seeing since... I didn't have time to think further. A lady had started to come towards us and, also with a smile, thrust a leaflet in our direction.

'Like what you see?' she said, as more of a statement than a question.

I tried to move away quickly whilst at the same time pulling at Shirley's hand.

'Come on,' I said purposefully, 'we've shopping to do.'.

Shirley pulled my hand back. 'Hang on, Pete. Look, dancing, I love dancing. Let's find out about this.'

Mild irritation now switched up a gear as my comfort zone was well and truly attacked. I hate dancing. In fact, on a list of things I hate most, dancing is up right there. *Jeez, I'm a bloke – get me out of here!* First shopping and now this!

I looked for a way out towards the relative safety of the fresh vegetable section just to my right. Yes; I had a sudden interest in what might be on the shopping list. But Shirley was now extending her free hand towards the leaflet and made eye contact with the lady. They were talking. The lady was telling Shirley about the classes and what night of the week they were on. Please, let it be any night but Thursday – my only free night…

'They're on Thursdays,' the lady said.

I needed to get Shirley away fast. It was time for some damage limitation: be a caring husband with the shopping; even offer to take her to look in the clothes section – and then get that leaflet out of her grasp and into the nearest bin. Then there'd just be the task of getting out past those damn dancers and down to the safety of the car park.

I went to work on that plan and we got home, but there were some aftershocks. Shirley did eventually prise herself away but not before one of the guys from the dancing group had taken her for a dance and put her through her paces. She didn't need much persuasion.

He'd taken her hand and guided her into the middle of the area they'd occupied for the dancing, and soon she was being led along to the next track of upbeat music, still with that smile on her face.

I took the shopping trolley off and hung around the vegetable section, looking across a few times to see Shirley laughing away with the dancing man. Why was she so happy? Still, good luck to them. I was safe in the knowledge it would all end in a few minutes and he could irritate some other people.

It seemed ages. I'd pushed that trolley round and round the same area before she finally decided to join me and I was not amused. Needless to say, I was in no mood for the look round the clothes section that I may have reluctantly agreed to earlier. In her state of happy excitement, Shirley eventually managed to find the shopping list in her back pocket and away we went.

All the way home Shirley was hyped up and went on and on about the dance she'd just had with 'Terry'. There was a way she said his name that, just for a second, made me uneasy.

In my head, I decided to rename him 'ponce bloke'. Did I care a damn? Did I heck! Football and drinks with the lads beckoned now so all this would soon be just a bad memory.

We carried the shopping in from the car with no words. Caroline had been waiting impatiently for her mum to get home as she wanted to bend her ear about her boyfriend's latest behaviour the night before. Normally that would have annoyed me but today it was a perfect distraction to get Shirleys mind back on her usual routine and duties. As far as I was concerned, that awful morning in the supermarket ended there and then and would not be mentioned again.

Perhaps it had just slipped my mind but... she still had the leaflet!

I woke up the following morning and slowly the events of Saturday started to flash through my mind. I was alone in bed and could hear Shirley downstairs, talking annoyingly loudly to Amy. I had some making up to do and fast, as I remembered the night before!

Perhaps I did push it too much staying for those extra drinks but the Blues had lost and there had been much discussion to have in the pub afterwards. I'd not noticed the time creeping by. It was the wrong side of 1 am when I eventually rolled home in the taxi as I'd left the car in the pub car park. I hoped Shirley would be asleep and would have last looked at the clock well before midnight. So far so good, I thought as I slipped quietly into bed. Phew, I might just have got away with it.

Thirty seconds passed.

I then lost control, burped and broke wind.

Soon after, the silence was broken again by a frosty Shirley.

'You decided to come home, then.'

'Sorry, love, time just ran away and –'

I didn't have time to finish before Shirley brought this conversation to an abrupt and chilly end.

'I just want to sleep now… You pig.'

Twenty-two years of marriage had taught me how to handle situations like this and further conversation was not the answer. I soon dropped off to sleep, confidently thinking I would put things right in the morning.

The atmosphere was strained the rest of that weekend. Thank goodness Pat came round for coffee with Shirley so I was able to slip out and retrieve the car from the pub. Once there, I noticed a couple of friends from football were having a drink. I joined them for a swift one. Well, the drink was swift but the chat went on a bit. In fact, it was a great bit of therapy as talk turned to my experience in the supermarket the day before. Did we laugh! Quite rightly, we spent a good hour ridiculing anything and everything about dancing. My mate, Dave, got a bit carried away as he tried to impersonate John Travolta. The people in the pub loved it and I felt more confident than ever that we'd never be seen mixing with 'that lot' from yesterday.

I was still in a good frame of mind when I eventually arrived home. Walking in, I noticed the leaflet on the kitchen table. But I resisted the temptation to pick it up and take it somewhere I could throw it away. Looking back I so wish I had! The rest of the day passed uneventfully but I was a bit miffed when Shirley turned me down again when I tried it on once more in the bedroom that evening.

It was the next evening when I was off to the gym that Shirley seized her chance. I was just coming down the stairs with my bag and about to give her a quick kiss before heading off when she said…

'How about we try that dancing class this Thursday?'

I stopped dead in my tracks. 'Sorry?' I replied. I was taken completely off guard.

'The leaflet says it's free on the first night. It looks fun and if you don't like it there's no obligation to go again. What do you think?'

I hesitated for a few moments. Truth be told, I was fuming but did I think this would really go away so easily? No time for debate so I went for it with both barrels.

'What? No, love, you know it's not me. And we do enough, don't we? Your job keeps you busy and I work all week. Nice idea but, no!'

Shirley turned away. 'Sorry. I just thought it was something we could do together.'

No more to say and, in my mind, this closed the conversation. In a way, it was a relief to finally put the events of Saturday to bed. With that, I went off to the gym.

Tuesday mornings can be a real drag. That morning, however, I woke up relaxed after a heavy workout the night before. Maybe it was because I was still agitated by the dance thing that I'd put in an extra effort at the gym, but I was proud of my physique and knew it turned Shirley on. Also, that evening the Blues were playing at home in a weekday cup game.

Over breakfast, Shirley was more distant than usual but seemed to perk up when the girls came down and talk turned to their respective jobs and the day ahead. Amy worked in a fashion shop and Caroline in administration. Both were steady jobs but there was always a drama of some sort to chew over at breakfast and that day was no different. A routine day at work for me followed.

Well, I can't say it was a shock. Shirley had obviously had a bad day and, over dinner that evening, saw the opportunity to bring up Saturday night's late homecoming and how our marriage was 'all about me'. If I cared for her I would at least have considered trying out the dance class.

I wasn't in the mood for this. Football beckoned and here we were, back on the subject of *this* again. I thought I'd made my feelings clear last night. My head was in my hands when I gave in… for now.

'Ok, ok, you win! I'll go if that'll make you happy. Not this Thursday as I have a big job on at work and might be late home but maybe the week after.'

Shirley had a smile on her face so with a quick kiss I was off.

My mind had turned straight to the football and for then I'd bought time… precious time. She was happy and would shut up about this stupid dancing and I had well over a week to think of an excuse. By that next Thursday, there were going to be endless possibilities: Amy or Caroline might have broken up with their boyfriends or at least have some sort of crisis, thus completely distracting Shirley and of course needing her undivided attention. The car might have packed up, boiler broken down, fence blown down. A multitude of natural disasters had a chance of happening so why did I need to worry? Happy days, I thought.

But time has a habit of creeping up on you. Life went on and suddenly it was a week Thursday! How had that happened? Just routine and nothing out of the ordinary going on? On that Tuesday evening when I'd stupidly agreed, a week Thursday had seemed too far away to worry about. Yes, it had crossed my mind in a hazy, black, deeply depressing way every day since, but there had always been time… Ok, I'd buried my head in the sand. I'd tried to blot out thinking about *that evening.*

I arrived home from work and Shirley was full of the joys of spring, even on a cold and wet October night. Could I feign injury? Food poisoning? Please could a neighbour knock the door with a request for help, a phone call, ANYTHING… *please…* Amy and Caroline, along with their boyfriends, could normally always be depended on to need help that night, or what about Pat and her kids? Where were they all when I needed them a crisis?

There was no last-minute reprieve.

I was furious it had come to this and I let Shirley know by my mood as we left the house. She had of course done her homework and found out what we needed in terms of footwear. We were to stick with comfortable shoes for our first night. Just a casual dress code. No problem there for me but Shirley seemed to change at least three times before we got on our way. She offered to drive so I could have a drink, which was the least she could do in the circumstances. I even had a can of beer before we left to try to take the edge off. Some hope of that!

In we went, and the only bit of comfort was that there was a bar. I bought a pint for me and it was water for Shirley, then face the music. If only it had been just the music!

The class started with about fifty people, who had soon grown to over a hundred before the end of what the teacher cheerily called, 'the beginner routine'.

Still far from happy, I started dancing with Shirley, but things soon got progressively more challenging when everyone moved round and we had to dance with different partners every few minutes. I was met with a range of responses, from a warm and nice, 'Is it your first night? Oh, don't worry, you'll be fine and love it' to a near hostile, 'You're supposed to be leading me'.

Shirley, by contrast, had shot off and seemed blissfully cheerful.

I thought the evening was over when the class ended and everybody clapped the teachers on the stage. Show willingness, I thought, clap along. And I smiled through clenched teeth. Why was everybody so darn happy, including Shirley? Still, what the heck? The job was done here, mission completed. I'd fulfilled my obligation and promise to Shirl.

My mind was already racing ahead to getting home and catching the football highlights on the box. Yes, normality was resumed, thank goodness. I fumbled in my pockets for the car keys while I took what I thought was a last look at these annoying people, who were still in a state of happy excitement. Struth, how I hated them!

More irritating still was seeing Shirley clapping along so enthusiastically with them, smiling in a way I hadn't seen for a long time, but then realising it was the same happy smile

I'd seen a few weeks previously when we first came across the dancing at the supermarket.

Still, all this was irrelevant as we were off. I nearly broke into a smile myself as I pressed the remote on the car key fob, wondering if I could open the door and start the engine from that far away. Yes, that's how much I had wanted to get out of the place. At least I still had the car keys. Just habit, I suppose. I'd taken them from Shirley as soon as she'd locked the doors. For the first time that evening, I actually started to relax.

What happened then soon put paid to that…

'So, this is what happens next,' said the guy on the stage, clapping his hands loudly to draw everybody's attention. He'd been teaching the class with his lady demonstrator and she stood grinning at his side.

'As always, we have some new dancers tonight and we welcome them to the wonderful world of dance. So, after a short section of freestyle and a chance to grab yourselves a drink, there will be a follow-up coaching session for those beginners and those who have been coming for a few weeks. This will be in the back room with our lovely coaches who tonight are Bill… Pauline… Terry… and Yvonne…'

He had made a show of pointing them out where they stood and they all soaked up even more applause. Not the first time that night, I noticed one of them was the bloke Shirley had ended up dancing with at the supermarket. Yes, it was ponce bloke. He was already really getting on my nerves! Why? *He just was!*

The teacher carried on. 'The rest of you are welcome to join our intermediate class and after that, it's dance, dance and keep dancing through to 11 o'clock!'

My hand on the car keys had gone sweaty. Shirley looked across from another line of dancers where she had finished the class. She was mouthing across at me something that looked like, 'Fantastic, we can practise more!'

WHAT?? Nooo! This was not what I had agreed. It was just one class, right? Forty-five minutes tops, she'd said, just to see how we got on. End of. Finished. The job would be done and I'd be in Shirley's good books for ages.

But when I tried frantically to get her attention again, and things were getting really desperate as she was still chatting away far too enthusiastically to her partner, the teacher's voice broke out again.

'OK, it's into freestyle!'

As the music started, I became aware of a new problem. The lady I had finished the class with was staring at me. Was that a flirty smile or a friendly smile? I thought.

'Shall we carry on dancing?' she inquired.

Real panic now set in and more confusion raced through my already overloaded brain. She was a really good-looking lady, mid-thirties maybe and, during the brief few minutes I had been clumsily stepping the routine through to the music with her, I'd noticed a lovely fragrance of perfume that surrounded her. Add to that the short, black dress that showed off her lovely, slim legs, and the long, flowing blond hair, and this should have been every man's dream. So why wasn't it? Was it perhaps because she was going to have expectations I was not able to live up to in this environment? I had cringed as, during one of the moves in the routine, my hand had accidentally brushed one of her boobs.

'Sorry, love,' I'd mumbled.

'These things happen,' she'd responded with a little giggle, almost in sympathy I thought.

I felt uncomfortable. Worse still, I then spotted Shirley starting to dance with the guy she had ended the class with. Christ, she didn't need much encouragement, if any. I quickly turned my attention back to the lady, who was starting to look round the room.

'Sorry, love,' I mumbled, 'it's my first time here and I need a drink.'

I realised what a pathetic line this was but nothing else had come to mind. The lady shrugged her shoulders as I stumbled off the dance floor, narrowly missing people who had already started dancing.

Trying to avoid eye contact with anyone, I found our table, slumped down into my seat and grabbed my pint of beer, already half-empty from having to cope with the uncomfortable quarter of an hour when we'd first arrived. That seemed a lifetime ago. I then watched Shirley dancing, looking so comfortable and happy in those surroundings. I was praying for the dance to end and for Shirley to rescue me from the nightmare I was in. As I sat there, every second seemed like an hour of my life.

Suddenly, I remembered a lifeline: my mobile, which Shirley had told me to switch to silent before we'd got out of the car. I grabbed it from my pocket, entered the passcode and randomly scrolled through anything and everything. I felt I now had some sort of control over the situation in case, horror of horrors, anyone else came to speak to me or, worse still, ask me to dance. I clutched at my half-empty pint for comfort (how ironic as it couldn't possibly be half-full, not tonight) and I glared at the phone as if I was reading a so-important message.

I had the car keys ready to make a point of leaving as a backup. I'd even thought briefly of drinking up and going to buy another pint as the prices were remarkably reasonable, but I quickly dismissed the idea. That would have given the impression I wasn't ready to leave.

I glanced up and noticed the lady I'd refused being expertly led in moves that were far more advanced than the few I'd just spent all that time trying to master. But the guy she was with now looked ridiculous! Hardly any hair, shorts, grey socks and black dance shoes, and a pathetic, stupid grin on his face. He was almost dribbling with glee. To make matters worse, the lady looked happy and confident and I'm sure it was for my benefit when, as she got briefly flung into a move, she made a point of glancing over, her face clearly saying, 'Look who you dumped!' What the heck did she see in that stupid prat that could make her so happy?

Into my eyeline, and just to compound the evening's misery, entered the coach from the stage. Yes, it was ponce bloke again. He was dancing with another lady, who was lapping up the attention that she must have known was focused on the pair of them, as he smoothly led her into a move she seemed to enjoy. He paused with her in his arms, and then her long, dark hair whipped around and they smiled at one another in a state of happy pleasure.

At last the music stopped briefly and Shirley eventually headed back towards me. Surely my face told her it was time to go. But she had other ideas.

'Just the coaching session now,' she pleaded. 'We've come this far. Twenty more minutes and we can go home. Please, *please* just do this for me.'

So now we were in the coaching room, the last place on earth I wanted to be. I sat alone, slumped in the plastic chair in the corner, hoping and praying I could remain hidden until the pantomime was over. But no. Shirley was with the lady coach and was pointing in my direction... How had things come to this?

***

Time stood still. Then – snap! I was back in the room. Or in this case, back in the coaching room. The lady was getting nearer. Could I escape…?

Too late she was leaning over to speak.

'Hi, your wife says it's your first night. Well, we're here to help. Shall we get you up and go over tonight's routine at your pace? Absolutely nothing to worry about. Everybody has nerves the first night.'

I collected my thoughts as quickly as possible and went into survival mode: fight or flight but the door was too far away. In my case it was fight or flight or freeze. There was no escape so I made a strong case for my defence.

'No, it's ok. I just came along to support my wife and she seems happy as she is so I'll just sit and observe. But thanks anyway.' I was on a roll so I added, 'To be honest it's no good for me. I've got two left feet.' I smiled, thinking I'd just put forward a winning case.

I could already visualise her walking away and moving on to a more worthwhile cause.

Not likely… Not yet.

'So how do you walk with two left feet? More to the point, it must be very difficult buying shoes.'

I'd like to think this was sarcasm at its worst, but it seemed almost polite. Next round! I went for broke.

'No, you don't understand, love, I have no rhythm. I really do have two left feet and I can't hear a beat in the music. I'm a lost cause. It was a mistake coming but I'm ok sitting here while you guys finish with Shirley.'

I half expected her to give me a counselling leaflet or make a call for a team of people to rush in to help as my case was so unique. It had also crossed my mind that Shirley was doing quite all right without me. Not only was she laughing away with all the other poor souls but ponce bloke Terry was helping with the coaching, so again spending time with his new project.

This all took the pressure away. Or it should have done if Shirley hadn't looked over, noticed me in the corner and pointed me out to Pauline, the coach.

Pauline hesitated slightly, then continued, 'Ok, now we've got that all out the way, shall we make a start? Up you get, and I won't bite.'

The next half hour was a blur of more misery. How could anything so simple be so complicated? But then, with no interest whatsoever, I'd gone through the motions with one eye on the clock on the wall.

Pauline had the patience of a saint as she went over and over the night's routine with me, while offering encouragement and kind words. It wasn't her I had the problem with, it was the situation. I still found moments to glance over from time to time and spot Shirley with ponce bloke Terry, seemingly enjoying every minute.

Eventually, the session ended with more polite applause for the coaches and now, at last, the night was over. I did the decent thing and politely thanked Pauline, who continued to heap praise on me and finished with a closing shot:

'So, we will see you next week then?'

I couldn't work out if this was a statement or a question but either way, it wasn't worth a response, even if I could have thought of one that was remotely polite.

'Thanks again, love,' was all there was to be said, with a forced smile.

Now, where the heck was Shirley? As if I needed to guess. She was still chatting with Terry, this time with a small group of the others. I just managed to catch her attention long enough to give her a glare and a nod that left her in no doubt it was time to go. She said her goodbyes to the others and I noticed Terry lean in and kiss her on the cheek as she moved away. If that wasn't irritating enough, he had to come over and offer his hand to me, repeating almost word for word Pauline's parting comment. He only needed to say goodbye. I remember thinking that if I never saw him again it would be too soon.

On the journey home, Shirley was in a mood of almost hysterical joy. She twittered on while she drove and I sat, still peeved, but coming to terms with it now that the miserable experience was over. I didn't even bother to comment on her driving although her gear-changing was as awful as ever.

I never did watch football that evening. We arrived back to find Amy and Caroline were both out and, before I knew it, Shirley had dragged me upstairs for a very memorable experience! She was on fire. She needed a real man and I was able to oblige. The night ended and in our own ways, we were both happy.

***

We never went back...

So, life carried on. It's nearly a year later and my story picks up again on a Saturday afternoon in late August.

The Blues were playing away that day in London so not a game I would have considered going to. The sun shone down as I walked towards the betting shop in our local town. I'd just had a swift lunchtime pint and, before heading home, fancied having a cheeky little bet on the game later that afternoon. With my mind focused on this, I didn't notice somebody walking towards me.

'Ahhh, a guy, just what we need! Can I give you a leaflet about our dance club?'

An attractive lady with tight, ripped jeans, cropped top and long, dark hair was offering me a flyer.

'Don't be shy – you know you want to come and see,' she said, trying to draw my attention to the dancing in the precinct nearby.

There was normally music of some kind playing on a Saturday in town so it hadn't occurred to me the music I could hear was for a dance group, but there they were. And quite a group of them, too, dancing in couples.

Attractive as the lady was, I made my excuses.

'Sorry, love, places to be and all that.'

'Ok, but read the leaflet and hope to see you soon,' she replied, with a flirty smile that almost tempted me to carry on the conversation.

She was hot stuff, all right, but regaining my composure I hot-footed it to the betting shop. For a moment, the whole experience from the year before had flashed back. I'd been able to put it all behind me but the sight of the couples dancing in that familiar style and the lady approaching me had awakened a bad memory.

Maybe it was because it was such a lovely afternoon, but I was feeling quite chilled. Shirley wasn't with me and I sat on a bench in the precinct for a while. Making sure I was far enough away so as to not get any attention from the ladies who were still handing out leaflets, I watched. I don't know if they were the same group as before and frankly couldn't care, but the thought did cross my mind, along with wondering if old ponce bloke was there.

I distinctly remember having time to watch without any worries, knowing Shirley was with our girls at a shopping outlet twenty odd miles away. I observed and realised how right I was to have knocked the idea of us going back firmly into touch.

It occurred to me that, as a song finished, about ten spare ladies were waiting to pounce on the four or five guys dancing. They were dotted around the outside of the dance area, moving with the music, and as a song finished, they would rush towards the poor guys, who didn't even seem to have time to grab a drink! Hilarious, I thought. Even funnier was when the same ladies spotted a man walking towards the group. I wasn't sure if he was just out shopping or not but suddenly that was irrelevant as he was pulled into the dance area. It became obvious straightaway that he was experienced at dancing, as he seamlessly took the lady who had got there first through a series of moves that demonstrated he knew what he was doing. Poor sod, I thought, he only went out to the shops!

I was just thinking of heading home when, out from the other shoppers – yes, right on cue – ponce bloke himself arrived on the scene. He just had time to wave a few friendly greetings before a lady pounced, grabbed his hand and they started dancing. I remember thinking to myself that, if I was over there, I wouldn't know which bloke to punch first! Ridiculous, I know, but the thought made me happy.

Before I left to head home that day, I had one last look and then paused briefly to remind myself that Shirley and I had both moved on since that night at the dance class. No regrets, no problems and all forgotten. I was certainly never intending to mention this encounter. In fact, by the time I got home, I'd heard the Blues were three-nil up and I was thinking about my winnings!

You know, until that day I'd never really thought about it. But I suppose there was a little bit more that happened after that night at the dance class last year…

***

I'd hated that night; hated the whole thing, from that morning in the supermarket till the horrendous evening at the dance class. I'd thought it wouldn't happen and Shirley would get the message but she'd seemed determined to put me through it. I was so glad to get back to work and a bit of normality the next day but I think it was on Friday evening about a week later that things came to a head.

It must have been playing on Shirley's mind and she chose her timing to perfection, as the *Strictly* review programme was ending and I'd just finished my dinner.

'So, are we going to give the dancing another go next week?' she asked.

Well, I had to make a stand. And I was prepared to give her my view of things as I probably should have done a few weeks before this fiasco came about. A few home truths were needed and I gave her the lot.

She needed to have a reality check. I worked damn hard to pay the bills and keep the family in the life we had: holidays abroad, saving for both daughters' weddings, mortgage, including the conservatory extension that was added and that I'd just finished paying for a few months ago. Why did she want to put me through something I wasn't comfortable with? Surely she could see how I felt about it? She had her friends from work and was free to go out if she wanted. I probably said a whole lot more, too, as all my frustrations came out.

I think she got the message. She didn't offer a lot in terms of defence and what could she say anyway as I had her bang to rights? I suppose she may have mumbled something about us 'doing something together'. But she'd said this before and I'd struggled to work out her logic. Why would she want to come to football and she'd never mentioned coming to the gym? We had a holiday together every year...

Maybe that was something to discuss another day. Yes, sorted, and I didn't have to waste another minute of my life thinking about dancing.

So, life returned to normal and no more was said. Shirley enjoyed her Saturday evenings watching *Strictly* and early the next year went with both daughters and some of her friends to a *Strictly* tour show in London. She desperately wanted me to go with her but it clashed with a midweek game and that, of course, made it a no-brainer. This had been a blessing though as otherwise, I might have had to sit through it and the very thought leaves me cold.

Caroline's boyfriend went with them and I admit I did give him some grief for that. Perhaps I did go a bit far by suggesting ponce bloke from the dance class might be there, and Shirley gave me a look of disgust!

There were some other times dancing reared its ugly head and caused a few uneasy moments but on the whole, I always managed to bat them off without too much trouble.

It was the next summer that we were booked to go on a cruise to the Canaries. Shirley had always wanted a cruise holiday but this wasn't my cup of tea at all. Perhaps it was still a bit of guilt about the dancing and I thought this would get me back in Shirley's good books.

It was ok on the whole, out of the football season and drinks package included, and I soon found some guys to talk football with while Shirley soaked up the rays on the sunbed. We got friendly with quite a few couples and, on the port days when we went ashore, I would often find a drinking hole with the chaps while Shirley would go sightseeing or shopping with the ladies. We soon got into a routine and all was good.

But everything seems to have a downside. Unfortunately for me, they taught dance classes on the ship. As Shirley read the daily programme, just for a minute I saw that smile rush across her face when she read it out. One look at *my* face was enough to make the smile to disappear. That was a no, then.

I used to watch the class from the bar sometimes and almost delighted in seeing the agony on the faces of the guys who had been dragged up, kicking and screaming. They stumbled around, almost falling over their own feet while the ladies tried their best to make them move. I felt their misery as I had long, enjoyable swigs of my lager.

There were ladies spare without partners. Some tried to beckon their fellas up without any luck. The teacher often asked if any men watching would like to join in. Fat chance!

Then there were the evenings. There was a party band playing and, during each set, they would play a range of popular music. Annoyingly, there were a few couples who could dance very well and, worse still, in that style that had caused all the upset last year. Yes, Shirley had noticed. She looked on tapping her feet, transfixed. She thought better than to say anything but I could see how much she loved it. I had no problem at all with her *watching* all she liked.

It was one night when I snapped. I'd downed a few more beers than normal and one of the couples were up strutting their stuff. I don't know what came over me but before I knew it, I'd decided to get up on the floor and crack off a few moves of my own. In the process, I wasn't aware how close I'd got to them. As a few more people joined the dance floor, I really went for it. John Travolta, eat your heart out.

I beckoned Shirley to join me. This is all her dreams come true, I thought. She was laughing but for some reason didn't budge. The dancing couple meanwhile had left the floor. Result, thought.

I remember an awkward moment one afternoon when we were leaving the restaurant on the ship after a lovely midday lunch. Shirley suddenly diverted slightly to speak to a couple who had just walked past us. The conversation that started was friendly enough with smiles, but I soon realised Shirley was praising them on their dancing. It dawned on me that they were one of the couples I'd seen in the evenings dancing to the party band. With that, I hung back from joining her and instead moved away, took the daily cruise programme out of my pocket and studied the activities for the rest of the day. After a short while, Shirley rejoined me. But her mood had suddenly changed and she was quite distant.

'What was that all about, then?' I asked.

'Well, you didn't bother coming over to find out, did you?

'Shirl, love… I thought I heard you talking about dancing so I left you to it.'

'Yeah… I guess that sums it up really. Let's just leave it, shall we?'

'Ok, if that's what you want,' I replied.

I intended pressing Shirley more but things moved on and any conversation involving dancing was never really worth the effort for all the grief it caused. But this still crosses my mind from time to time and one day, I must ask Shirley what happened back then.

***

The only other time I can recall dancing being an issue in our lives is the occasional social event. The most significant one that springs to mind was our daughter Caroline's engagement party last November.

If I remember, it was a couple from Dave's (Caroline's fiancé's) side of the family that caused the problem that night. We'd not met them before and not been introduced so it made it easier for me to take a dislike to them when they were annoyingly good dancers.

It was a successful party on the whole. We'd hired the local Community Centre and a DJ, and I was happy to mingle at the bar. Everybody seemed to be enjoying the evening and, as the drink flowed, the dance floor filled. Shirley seemed to be in a particularly happy mood and joined in the dancing. I vaguely remember watching as she bopped along with the other ladies to the normal type of party music.

Now and again, there was a whoop of joy as the DJ announced a song that sent them into a frenzy of excitement. Luckily, there were enough guys around to talk about the football that had been on earlier that day.

It must have been near the end of the evening when the DJ decided to play one of those irritating party songs that made me grind my teeth. Amy had just collected a drink from the bar and was eager to rejoin the fun. She made time to nudge me and point out a solitary guy on the dance floor amongst the ladies.

'What a mover!' she shouted to make herself heard above the music.

'What a prat!' seemed to come out of my mouth without any effort.

'Dad!' Amy looked horrified. 'Don't be so damned rude! Can you move like that?'

With that, she was off to join them but the exchange left me in a bad mood. I'd noticed the guy in question at different times during that evening. Mostly he'd been dancing with the lady he came with. While the majority of guests were just jigging along to the music, they'd been dancing in what looked similar to that jive-class style that was still a bad memory from a few months earlier. I didn't need a reminder. Now and again, I'd seen him dance with other ladies and once even with Shirley. I'd been chatting away so these had only been brief glances but now Amy had said this, it just rattled me.

It was then I wished I'd paid more attention when he was dancing with Shirley. What I could remember was that he'd made Shirley look good and I had to have a second glance to check it was her. Still, what the heck? He'd danced with a lot of the ladies so was this a problem? As long as he'd not got any ideas and tried it on with my woman. No one would ever do that. End of. Shirl and I had been together since we'd met at a nightclub when we were in our teens. For both of us, it was our first serious relationship after a few girlfriends on my part, and I think Shirl had had a few boyfriends, though she never really mentioned them. It had seemed so natural drifting from engagement to marriage, just like all our friends at the time. We were solid all right.

Anyway, I should have just left it there. He'd done nothing to me but again, this had really annoyed me and I needed to make a stand. I suppose the alcohol had a part to play. Come that time of the evening, I was well lubricated when I saw the opportunity to make my move. It's occurred to me since it was the same sort of red mist that had descended on me on the cruise ship. I was determined to be the one in charge of the situation.

A lot of the guests had started to leave and the dance floor was not so hectic. The couple in question were still up strutting their stuff. There were small groups of ladies dancing too, but I decided I'd like to have a few walks across the dance floor. I planned to intimidate. To walk as close as I could to the couple in the hope they'd not be aware and bump into me. I was braced for a collision and relished the thought of sending him or her sprawling. I intended to say sorry, even with a grin.

Sad to say, I had no joy. After three of four attempts, I went back to the bar. They left the floor anyway so I suppose I had a bit of a result.

I never see the problem with those sorts of nights. Shirley can dance if she wants. I'm happy with a beer and a chat; a game of pool or darts perhaps. Why would I want to dance? It's not a man thing anyway.

***

So, there you have it. I was asked if I'd go dancing and I guess this story sums it up but I will make a few points absolutely clear.

Do I ever give it another thought? No. And I wasn't going to until it came up in the pub and brought it all back. All this has nothing to do with our marriage. I love Shirley and she loves me. Fact!

Yep, everything is rosy in the garden and life is good. I often wish I knew what the heck Shirley was thinking but should I worry about that? Not a chance. She knows when she's well off. Till death do us part it is and happy days!

Shirley's Story

'So why don't you and Pete go dancing then?' Pat asked.

I felt the tears welling up in my eyes as I looked for an answer.

Pat was my best friend and we'd been having one of our routine coffee mornings. We'd covered all the normal stuff and almost inevitably talk had moved on to *Strictly Come Dancing*. It had started again on the telly and we had our views on all the week's news and scandal. One thing was for sure – we both loved the whole dance experience.

During a pause as I'd gone to turn the kettle on for fresh drinks, her question had come out of the blue and hit me like a steam train.

'So, why not?' she repeated as I sat back down. Then, 'Shirley! What's wrong? What's brought this on?' She'd noticed the tears.

I had to tread carefully as Pat had lost her husband a few years back and there were often awkward situations. Pat had nobody to take her dancing – I did. But… And there lay the problem.

I quickly composed myself and lied about my tears being to do with an argument with Peter the night before. We seemed to be having disagreements regularly and the root of it all was not a million miles away from why this question had touched a nerve. I wasn't sure if Pat believed me but I didn't want to go there.

Later on, as I sat alone, the memories from the last year came flooding back. No, Pete and I don't go dancing…

***

I slumped down on the bed and cried my eyes out, angry and frustrated at the same time. Boy, did I feel sorry for myself that afternoon in the cabin.

In the summer, we'd been on a cruise to the Canaries, just the two of us. I'd always fancied a cruise and Pete had finally gone for it. I thought this holiday was going to be a turning point, as things had become strained in the last few years.

Our daughters were grown up and independent and I wanted to spend some quality time with Pete. Was that too much to ask? Pete seemed to have his life all mapped out. Work, the gym, football and drinking with his friends. I was becoming invisible apart from his once-a-week interest in me for sex. Yes, making love had now become routine sex for his self-gratification! I wondered if he noticed my face sometimes. Did it look as if I was in the fires of passion?

Was I kidding myself when I thought this cruise would mend everything? Perhaps he'd actually noticed I was fed up. I was just pleased he seemed to initiate the idea and, of course, I jumped at it. In no time the holiday came round and we were boarding the ship.

It wasn't long, though, before Pete slipped into a routine. We soon met up with some couples that were easy to get on with, which in itself was fine. Pete, however, ended up disappearing with the guys for drinking sessions while I was left with the ladies. Pleasant as this was, I found myself getting frustrated as, again, we weren't spending any time together. I was surprised how much there was to do on the ship and, with being at sea for long periods, this should have been a chance to get to know one another all over again. Fat chance of that!

There were even dance lessons. It was the first morning and I'd been reading the daily programme as Pete took a shower. On seeing these advertised, a rush of anticipation vanished in a flicker as I remembered the experience from the year before. More on that later but as he was getting dressed, I thought it was at least worth a try.

'Look, Pete, cooking demonstration at 10 this morning and… a beginners' waltz class at 11.30. What do you think?'

'So that's you sorted then, love,' he said. 'Last night at dinner one of the guys mentioned a darts competition today. Is that in the programme?'

Of course, I'd noticed it. It was at 11 am, so no chance of making the dance class. I pretended to look even though I was staring straight at it.

'Oh, here it is. Yes, 11 am on deck 6. Darts tournament, round one.'

I looked up from the programme, paused, and had one last go at what I knew in my heart was a lost cause.

'So, you don't fancy coming with me to the dance class?'

'Shirl, why would I want to do that? You go. I'll come and meet you later and we can have some lunch.'

It wasn't just what he said but the look that went with it. The resignation hit me there and then on day one.

I went to the waltz class on my own. I felt awkward when I had to raise my hand so the teacher could identify me, along with about ten other ladies without partners in the class. There were dance hosts – a man and a lady. The lady had to take the man's role because of the surplus of ladies in the class.

That meant I ended up getting a turn about every fourth go. The other times I just watched, feeling really angry that Pete was on the same ship but wanted to be elsewhere. But I was grateful for the times when I was able to dance, especially with the male dance host, who seemed overworked as there were so many ladies! He was good though, and just for those brief few minutes, I felt a million dollars as he led me gracefully through the short routine we'd been taught.

'That was great, you're a natural,' he said with a broad smile.

'Thank you. And you led me really well,' I replied, wishing he would stay with me. But with another smile, he was off to the next grateful lady.

In between times, I remember watching the other couples and thinking how hard the men were trying but at least they were having a go. And then there were the couples that could obviously dance. They looked so comfortable and happy.

Did I envy them or did I hate them? Both!

As the class was ending, I noticed Pete. He was leaning up against a pillar near the bar, pint in hand. He was chatting to another man, not even bothering to look over at where I was. Yes, I stood on my own. No partner for me as the class was over and the routine was danced to music for the last time.

I hated Pete for that.

I hated him again a few days later. It sounds a terrible thing to say about someone you love. I often had to check myself, time and time again. How had this happened? When did it start? Why did he do these things? Why did he treat me with so little respect anymore? Was it me?

And that's where I ended up. Yes, it was me. I was being a right stroppy cow. But, yes, I did hate him that afternoon.

We'd returned from a morning trip to Santa Cruz in Tenerife. I'd not been in the best of moods because of Pete's actions. We left the ship early and discussed the possibility of finding a tourist trip from many of the local tour firms that would be waiting around the port. Before we had the chance, however, we bumped into one of the couples again and soon started to drift into town. My trip was becoming less likely by the minute. Then the guys began talking football and spotted a bar that was showing a sports show.

'How about you two go round the shops and we'll meet you back here in a few hours?' Pete said.

Brilliant! It's not that I had a problem with the lady. I just wanted Pete and me to spend some time together and make some memories. Was it too much to ask?

Anyway, that was our time gone. The ship sailed at 4 pm so it was back for dinner and an afternoon on the sun loungers.

'Who's going to join us for this afternoon's Salsa class?'

I raised my head to see a couple from the entertainment team at the front of the pool area, where they had a sectioned off the space prepared for a dance class.

Latin music filled the air. Immediately, you could see people moving their arms and tapping their feet to the rhythm. It was the sort of music that lifted your mood in an instant and lent itself so well to the sunshine that was beating down. I really wanted to be a part of this.

'There you are, love, just your cup of tea.'

Pete didn't seem to move a muscle as these words came out. But with that simple sentence, he managed yet again to bring my mood crashing down in an instant.

'Are you going to join me, then?' I asked, with more than a hint of sarcasm as I leaned across towards his sunbed. He looked up briefly and gave me a cold stare.

'That's a no, then. Thanks a lot,' I replied.

Sod him! I decided at that point that I would join in.

I remember the slightly awkward walk through the other sunbeds until I joined the rest of the ladies who had started to gather round near the dance couple. They were a couple from the show team who performed in the evenings in the main theatre. Both barely out of their teens with perfect, tanned bodies. But that didn't seem to tempt any of the men around the pool to join us.

'So, we need more men. Come on, these lovely ladies need you.'

As the guy made the futile request, his partner quickly made her way round the sunbeds, trying in vain to coax up one of the many men. No chance. They were having none of it. I threw a stare across at Pete but he was oblivious. So we started with about twenty ladies and three men, soon down to two as one swiftly scurried off.

Realising this was not going to work in couples, the teachers turned it into more of a line dance class and that was great fun. Along with the other ladies, I really enjoyed moving my body to the Latin beat. What's not to love?

In a break in the music, I cast another glance at Pete as he sat, drinking his beer. I then took a look at all the other men slumped around the pool. A few were looking at the young lady dance teacher, trying hard not to make it to obvious. But it was even so, and quite pathetic I thought. What is it they don't get about women loving to dance? They seemed totally unaware of the attention the two men who had joined the class were getting. And was I jealous of their partners. Lucky cows!

After dinner every evening it was off to the show. Following on would be a mixture of game shows and quizzes. The night would always end with us watching the party band with our new friends. And, of course, there was always dancing. I loved watching and occasionally joining in and having a bop while Pete looked on. It's funny how you really remember the good dancers. There were quite a few couples who often danced together those evenings and there was one couple in particular that had taken my eye. They were about our age group and danced modern jive to many of the songs, not only when the group played but during the breaks when the DJ took over. They looked so happy together and so in tune with the music and one another.

One particular night, Pete was chatting away with his friend, Frank, while I sat watching the dancing with Frank's wife, Jane. I noticed her watching the same couple as she leaned in to speak above the music.

'Aren't they great dancers, Shirley?'

'Oh, yes,' I replied. 'I just love watching them. Come on, do you fancy getting up and having a dance?'

Jane didn't need asking twice and we took to the floor and bopped around while all the time I had one eye on the dancing couple.

Later in the evening, things took an embarrassing turn.

After Jane and I had enjoyed a few dances, we carried on chatting happily, occasionally sharing the odd words with our fellas. As normal, the drinks flowed, especially for Pete, who seemed hell-bent on taking advantage of the all-inclusive package.

Jane and I were chatting and watching the dancing again when suddenly, Pete jumped up and walked quite purposefully onto the dance floor. I didn't know what to say or think at this point. He started doing the most ridiculous dad dancing you could imagine. Frank joined him, thank goodness, and was a little less energetic. It wasn't long before a lot of the dancers left the floor, probably worried about their safety. I couldn't believe it when he tried to get me to join him. I really didn't know whether to laugh or cry. In the end, Jane started giggling and I couldn't help but join her. But inside I was furious.

'They could do with some lessons,' Jane said.

If only she knew. 'I'll tell you a story about that another time,' I promised.

That night back in the cabin, Pete and I had words again. So, he could act the fool on a dance floor but not do the one thing I wanted and spend time learning how to dance properly with me? Jane's words had hurt me and brought things to a head and I was furious. Pete laughed it all off – it was me overreacting again – and he seemed oblivious to why I was upset. It was a good job we were in twin beds on the ship as I really didn't want him near me that night.

The next day, I was able to follow up on my promise to Jane. Pete and Frank were at darts again and we treated ourselves to a cocktail by the pool. Aware that I'd probably not see Jane again after the cruise, what had I got to lose by sharing the story of last year's dance class? It certainly helped me, and Jane listened with interest as I unburdened my frustrations. I kept to the point and left out the personal detail, but I remembered those couple of weeks so well...

***

It was that morning in the supermarket. That day had been a real wake-up call. I hadn't noticed how much of a rut I'd got into. In fact, even that Saturday morning started so predictably. I'd just woken up as Pete started fumbling at my nightdress. He was after sex. Welcome to the weekend, I thought. His idea of lovemaking would be a quick 'wham, bam, thank you, mam'. With hardly a word exchanged, this would be followed by a shower and down to breakfast. Well, I just wasn't in the mood and I let him know.

The day didn't get any better when Pat called and cancelled the shopping trip we had planned for that morning.

Oh, well, I thought. Pete can help with the food shop this week. About time he got involved and it'll probably be the only time I'll get to spend with him this weekend.

The only saving grace was that *Strictly* was on telly that night and I did enjoy watching with Caroline and Amy over a glass of wine and some nibbles.

The thought of this perked me up a little and on the trip to the shops, I found myself chatting away about this year's contestants. One of them was an ex-footballer. I thought this might at least interest Pete. No chance! Football was on the radio and I suddenly realised he wasn't listening. I carried on talking and, without a break, suddenly slipped him a curveball at the end…

'So I reckon he'll last to about week four at the most but I think Pat and I will go out tonight and pick up a few blokes, then take them back to her place for some fun. What do you think, Pete?'

'Yeah, whatever you say, love,' he replied, while obviously straining to hear what was being said on the radio.

Needless to say, I was not in the best of moods when we arrived at the supermarket. Why was I noticing so many examples of why I was fed up with Pete?

But something special happened as we entered the supermarket that morning. All my frustrations were suddenly forgotten when I heard the music and saw the dancing. Even shopping could wait when we were greeted with the sight of a dance group busking as we went in.

We were handed a leaflet for a free dance lesson. The lady gave such a warm smile as she asked if we liked what we saw. Of course I did! This was a dream come true and something Pete and I could do together. This could be the future I was looking for right here.

Pete, however, did his best to put the dampers on and suddenly seemed very interested in the shopping. One of the men from the club came over to join the conversation and that was Pete's cue to clear off with the trolley.

'How about we have a dance?' the man asked.

For a second I froze – but only for a second. Then I replied, 'I haven't done it before. I only dance at parties.'

'Haven't done it before'? I still cringe now at how pathetic that must have sounded!

I soon forgot about it, though, as the man extended his hand. And I didn't need a second invitation. He led me to the middle of the floor and offered his other hand for me to take.

'Just follow my lead, feel the music, but most importantly, keep that smile and enjoy the dance,' he said, as he started to gently move my arms. His body movement seemed to bring my body to life and, without effort, I was dancing.

As he moved, he appeared to glide around the floor, and I found my hands switching effortlessly between his as I seemed to know instinctively what he was expecting of me.

I remember thinking how safe I felt and at the same time, what a most amazing experience. His lead became lighter still but he was giving me all I wanted from him. I've heard it said since that in a dance, it's the man's job to make sure the lady has a most enjoyable three minutes. I knew when I heard this that this was what had happened that day.

I didn't realise I was smiling so much, but this was so wonderful, I guess my face must have been showing it.

The music stopped too soon for me but, as it did, the man seemed to lead me into a position where we finished on the beat. Our bodies swayed slowly as the song ended. Pure bliss!

I closed my eyes and allowed myself a second to savour that moment. Would I experience this again? I could wish. And with Pete? I could wish… And believe me, in that fleeting moment, I did wish with all my heart.

'That was wonderful. How did it feel for you?' the man asked with a warm smile. 'I'm Terry, by the way, and I'm a coach at the club.'

'I really enjoyed it,' I replied, adding, 'I'm sorry if I messed up sometimes,' as I remembered a few times I'd turned the wrong way and he had expertly repositioned me without it going badly wrong. 'I'm Shirley.'

'Well, Shirley, I look forward to seeing you on a Thursday evening soon. Go on, after that lovely dance, tell me you've danced before?'

I laughed as he asked the question. Inwardly I was flattered. This man was complimenting me. He made me feel special. I felt so alive.

Suddenly, I snapped out of my happy bubble. Where was Pete? How long had I been dancing? I thanked Terry one more time, smiled at the lady handing out the leaflets and looked out into the shoppers. I soon spotted Pete. He was still in the vegetable section, leaning up against the trolley with a face like thunder. Before heading towards him I made sure I did one last important task: I checked the leaflet was safely in my pocket where I'd quickly put it when I was asked to dance.

I finished the shopping on automatic pilot with Pete sulking around behind me, pushing the trolley as if it weighed a ton. Sod it, I thought. He wasn't going to ruin my mood and, just for good measure on the way home, I mentioned how much I enjoyed the dance with Terry.

It seemed I had to pay for that brief, happy experience as the rest of the weekend returned to the same old mundane routine. But I enjoyed watching *Strictly* with the girls that evening. It brought the memory of the morning back into focus and, just for a few fleeting moments, I imagined a new chapter of my life beginning with Pete. As if I needed reminding how much I loved to dance.

That was as good as it got, though. Pete came home late from the pub that night. I'd got used to the Saturday football and even a drink afterwards with his mates, but that night he pushed it to a new level. I was woken by him clumsily clambering into bed and then making the most disgusting noises. Yes, I was used to it but that night it just got to me. Twenty-two years of marriage and this was my lot.

The next day I was able to bend Pat's ear when she came round for a coffee. She was a real friend and I could confide in her but even that went wrong that day. I was moaning about the day before and Pat suddenly went quiet.

'I wish I still had a husband I could moan about,' she said.

'Oh, Pat, I'm so sorry,' I answered 'I've been going on and on!'

With a hug, all was forgotten. This happened from time to time and I just needed to check myself. Pat was brilliant.

We seemed to chat for ages as, yet again, Pete had disappeared. He'd gone to fetch the car from the pub car park where he'd left it the night before. Twenty minutes' walk and five minutes' drive back but well over two hours passed before he came home.

'Shirley,' Pat said, as this had come up during my moan. 'Have you ever thought…?'

She gave me a long, penetrating look before I snapped back as politely as I could. 'Thought what? Another woman? Oh, God, no! It really is football and his mates.'

I thought this might be Pat's way of kicking back at me and, dare I say it, just a tad of jealousy.

'Anyway,' I went on, 'I'm going to get him to this dancing if it kills me.'

Yes, of course, I did briefly give it some thought but quickly dismissed the idea. Pete and another woman? I might be sick of him but he wouldn't do that. We were both completely committed to our wedding vows, of that I was sure.

I kept reminding myself about the dancing. I kept looking at the leaflet on the kitchen table. I had to find a way to get Pete to that class. Not that day, though. I'd got myself in a state and was just not in the mood for any further discussions with him.

He must have been in a state of blissful ignorance because that night, he came to bed thinking he was going to make love to me. He seemed really upset when I spurned his advances. He still didn't get it.

On the Monday morning, I woke with a new determination. I'd already started dreaming about Thursday. I found myself fantasising about being on the dance floor with Pete. I kept reliving how I'd felt during that dance on the Saturday. I could still hear the music. I wanted that feeling again.

I was working at the hairdressers in the morning and I felt a new spring in my step. I had a few regulars on a Monday and talk turned to *Strictly* as normal, but I couldn't help dropping in about what had happened on Saturday. And I found myself talking about the forthcoming Thursday as if it had already been agreed.

But it was never going to be as easy as that, was it?

I made my move that evening, just as Pete was off to the gym. Planned to perfection, I thought. He was off to his *beloved* gym. My work had gone well in the morning and I'd enjoyed the chats with the ladies as I worked on their hair. I'd done some housework in the afternoon and was just in the mood for my *Dirty Dancing* CD. What was I thinking about being this happy on a Monday afternoon?

So I asked, nicely, 'Could we try out that dancing class Thursday?'

Needless to say, it didn't go well. My earlier good mood was brought crashing down. Within a few painful minutes I was reminded of my role in this marriage. How stupid was I to think it would be nice to do something together.

Still, I brushed myself down and decided to have another go.

After breakfast the next morning, I was washing up and, thank goodness, something stirred inside me. I'd just spent the entire breakfast time waiting on and listening to Caroline, Amy and Pete: the trials and tribulations of their jobs, their boyfriends, Caroline's forthcoming engagement, and Pete showing us all his abs after his hard night at the gym.

Did I hear… 'So how are you, Mum?… What are you up to today?... Your hair looks nice this morning… Thanks for getting my breakfast ready… Can I give you a hand with anything?…'

Of course not. I was 'Mum' and 'wife' but God forbid I'd actually have anything to say worth listening to. Chief cook and bottle washer and available for sex on tap as needed.

So, they'd all got up from the breakfast table, left everything where it was and gone. Was it any wonder as I was washing up that I got angry? That last Saturday morning I'd seen something that could give me a life. And I wanted it to be with Pete. So, yes, I got angry. By dinner time that evening, I was ready to deliver a few home truths of my own…

And Pete agreed! That's all I needed. A commitment to go. Ok, it was for the week after rather than this Thursday, but he'd said yes. Looking back, maybe I should have realised he was rushing off to football. But at least I had something to cling on to.

For the next two weeks, I went round with a smile on my face. My dream was coming alive. I counted down the days to class night. During that time, I didn't mind being talked at as opposed to having a meaningful conversation. I didn't mind running around after everyone for no thanks. I even succumbed to Pete in the bedroom as I dared to believe he cared for me enough to want to come dancing with me.

As the day approached, however, he seemed to become more and more distant and I remember having a horrible feeling he was going to cry off. My mood switched from happy excitement one minute to low the next, as I imagined him coming up with an excuse. I almost resigned myself to the fact this would happen.

When Thursday eventually arrived, I somehow got through it. As soon as I got home from work I called the number on the leaflet to check on the dress code and footwear. It was also an excuse to speak to someone to check the class was on that night. A friendly lady answered my queries, then said she'd look out for us. My excitement was building so, when Pete arrived home, he must have sensed how joyous I was.

The girls seemed uneasy at my happy mood over dinner but, along with Pete's sulking, I wasn't going to let anything bother me. Amy and Caroline soon disappeared with looks I could read like a book: *Mum's happy; mum's very direct and positive in her advice tonight. How weird. Still, she'll be back to normal tomorrow.*

Pete went straight to the fridge, got a beer and disappeared into the lounge. I'll do the dishes, then. No change there but that night, I really didn't care.

Although I was told it was a class night so casual clothing, I made an effort. This was a date night with Pete and I wanted him to notice me. Make-up and perfume: `Youth Dew`, which was Pete's favourite. I'd not had that out for some time but I remember Pete used to say I smelt lovely. So, as he sat watching the early evening news, I went to work.

Looking back now, I cringe as I remember more details of that night. Earlier in the week, I'd been shopping for some new clothes for the class. I'd bought black trousers and jeans. I tried both on now with different tops and, looking in the mirror, with my mood that evening I liked what I saw. I'd not felt this good about myself in a long time. So why didn't Pete notice? I had to go downstairs at least twice to get things from the kitchen and all but walked straight across his eyeline.

Nothing.

And on the way out to the car. Nothing.

If I'd gone down in my frilliest knickers, stockings and suspenders, would he have noticed me then, I wonder?

I offered to drive that night. My logic was that Pete could have a beer to settle him down. Although I drove the short distance to work, Pete did the majority of the driving these days. Just another routine we'd had for as long as I could remember. Add to that the fact I didn't appreciate his constant moaning about my driving; it was more trouble than it was worth. But that evening he hardly said a word on either journey.

The night itself was all I could have wished for. After starting the class with Pete, we then moved around, which I had no problem with but I could see his discomfort. We had to learn, though, and what better way?

During the class, I came across all levels of ability, as well as Terry, who was a coach that evening. He was so pleased to see me and I felt a genuine warmth as he welcomed me with a gentle kiss on the cheek.

'Shirley, so happy you made it,' he said. 'When you weren't here last week, I did wonder if you'd had second thoughts.'

I shook my head. 'Not at all. It was a work thing with my husband. Lovely to see you again.'

'Well, that's it now,' he replied. 'You'll be hooked from tonight and I for one will be delighted with that. You're a natural. I knew it from that lovely dance we had the other week.'

Before we could say any more, the teacher was calling the moves and I knew I was in good hands.

I saw more of Terry later that night in the coaching room. I think he'd taken a shine to me after our meeting at the supermarket and could obviously see how enthusiastic I was. Although there was quite a crowd taking advantage of the extra coaching, he spent some time with me going over the moves and giving me hints and tips. I certainly didn't complain.

If the class was fun, how it ended was the icing on the cake. I finished the evening with a guy who was a very experienced dancer. I knew this as he led me through the moves and it was the last time we went straight into freestyle. It was absolute bliss.

'It's my first night,' I said nervously. 'I'll only be able to do tonight's moves.'

'That's absolutely no problem,' the man replied. 'A few times and then we'll see. Just trust me, ok?'

The way he said it, along with his smile, convinced me, and I returned the smile. 'I'm in your hands.'

I seemed to know exactly where to go without him having to use any force to lead me. I couldn't tell you what we did in terms of any moves but we were really dancing. Afterwards I basked in the afterglow. I felt fulfilled. I wanted more of this. I don't remember his name but I wouldn't forget him in a hurry!

I finished the dance with the same warm glow I'd experienced in the supermarket with Terry. But with that came another familiar feeling. Where was Pete? How long had I been dancing? I'm sure the guy wanted to chat more but I panicked, gave him a nervous smile and was off. I think back now and curse myself for not thanking him for that dance. But I was in a state. I hadn't realised that, at the end of the class, the teacher would announce there was a coaching session available afterwards. I looked across to Pete and tried to indicate this was a great opportunity. Then, of course, I lost myself in the dance. Only now I had to go and face the music.

I made my way quickly back to where we'd been sitting before the class started. Pete's face was like thunder, but we'd come this far and I was determined to squeeze all I could out of the evening.

We did get out into the coaching room and it was embarrassing when I had caught him sitting in the corner of the room, sulking like a naughty schoolboy. One of the coaches was the lady who'd been so supportive at the supermarket and I asked her if she could help. She was brilliant with him. I was sure this was just the kickstart he needed. I even thought I saw him perk up a bit in the times I glanced over. As you can imagine, I was in my element. And once Pete was sorted, I was back to concentrating on Terry and the others.

I loved that night! I felt reborn. So full of life. From being an old-before-my-time mum with a mundane job, listening to everyone else and their lovely lives and fetching and carrying for everyone, suddenly I felt a teenager again. So many possibilities flashed before me. My mind wandered off with so many aspirations. I watched couples dancing together, so in tune with one another, smiling and laughing as they did the most amazing moves. Others weren't so good, but they still had those infectious smiles, stopping as the lady was reduced to fits of giggles when they got a move wrong and ended up with their arms twisted. I saw what were obviously proper couples, too, by the way they held hands and kissed, and I so envied them.

And, yes, I did imagine my Pete and me in six months doing these things in that happy, vibrant atmosphere.

If I close my eyes, I can still flick back in my mind and feel the positive emotions of that night. I drove home in a state of bliss and Pete didn't have to work hard to get me into the bedroom when we got back. I took control. This was my night…

The next week was a real mixed bag. One minute I'd be daydreaming of me, twirling around the floor, and the music would be playing in my head; the next I'd come crashing down to earth as I thought of the uphill struggle with my fella!

A moment presented itself on the Friday night. I think misery chops had just come in from work as the girls and I were watching the end of the Strictly highlights show.

He finished his dinner. With his belly full of beef stew and dumplings, I knew it was now or never. All I did was drop in as carefully as I could the possibility of giving the dancing another go next week. I was not prepared for the outburst that followed; I really seemed to have struck a nerve.

It was horrible being told it was my fault he had endured the most miserable week he could remember. He reminded me how lucky I was and to count my blessings. Let's just say I was put firmly in my place and it was pretty crystal clear this was the first and last time we would ever be going near a dance class again. Hell would freeze over were the words the conversation closed with.

The end. Finished.

I cried later that night after he stormed out and went to the gym. All the highs I'd felt the previous week were gone and replaced with what? And here I was, washing the dishes but of course realising how lucky I was in this lovely house with all the trappings of a wonderful family life.

Perhaps Pete had a point and I was being a cow. Did I push the boundaries too far? He worked hard; he provided; he was a wonderful husband to me and father to our daughters, and he loved us. What was I thinking putting him through that? But I just wanted us to do something together.

I think you could describe it as acceptance. He won't dance and that's just the way it is. I'll still always love dancing, but I do admit I can get really jealous when I see other people enjoying themselves on the dance floor. As for seeing actual couples together dancing, I hate them! How dare they be that happy?

***

'So,' I finished, glancing at Jane, 'I think you can establish from that we never did go back.'

Jane had been listening patiently. 'Welcome to my world,' she said. She held up her cocktail which by now was nearly empty.

'Oh, Jane, I'm so sorry. It must be the drink – I have gone on a bit.' I realised that although she'd been involved in the conversation, I'd really bent her ear for the last part of my story.

'At least you got him to a lesson. I somehow don't think I'd even get Frank that far.'

'Have you ever tried?' I asked. 'I can see you like dancing.' I spotted an opportunity to find out if I was alone in how I felt about all this.

'Don't be daft,' Jane replied with a chuckle. 'Pigs might fly before Frank would go dancing. But that's just the way he is.'

I didn't push the conversation any further with Jane. I could see she accepted the way things were. Shortly afterwards, she made her excuses as she had a treatment booked at the onboard beauty spa. As I lay on my sun lounger with another cocktail, I can remember so vividly having a long reflection on that chat.

'That's just the way he is,' Jane had said. And Pete's just the way *he* is. So that makes it all right then, does it? That makes it acceptable? I go out of my way to make sure Pete gets what he wants. I cook meals around his lifestyle. Who always gets their way when we change the car?

I've always wanted a Mini and last year, I thought for the first time I might get one. But no. Pete talked me round to the large SUV. 'You know it makes sense,' he said. Did it? I'd not thought to argue the case.

More and more examples kept coming into my head as I lay sipping my drink. While the children were growing up, who was their taxi driver? Good old Mum. Dad was always busy doing what Dad wanted. But he was still their hero of course. Mum was just the skivvy. That's what she did.

Finally that afternoon, my eye caught a couple on the sunbeds on the opposite side. I'd seen them on a few occasions around the ship and there was something that caught my attention every time: they weren't talking. Ok, so they were sunbathing together but I'd never seen them talk. They were older, perhaps late sixties, early seventies, and I'd often spotted them in various lounges, at shows and meal tables, but I swear I'd never seem them talking to one another. Occasionally I saw them wandering around the ship, the lady always a few paces behind the man. But I noticed them more today on the sunbeds because of something that had happened the evening before. It was at the early evening show. There was a comedian that night, a really funny man, and during the show he'd done the comedian thing and started picking on people randomly in the audience.

For some reason I can't remember, this couple had come to his attention as they were in the first few rows, and it transpired it was their wedding anniversary: 'Forty-five years, ladies and gentlemen! Let's give them a huge round of applause!'

Forty-five years, I'd thought! And when had they last spoken to each other? I know I was out of order as I didn't know them or their circumstances but I'd seen many *couples like this.* Of course, the woman would say, I'm sure, 'That's just the way he is...'

More to the point, I was seeing into the future. Suddenly, I saw Pete and me in twenty to thirty years' time. This led to an even worse thought. Only the day before we'd been in Lanzarote. We'd taken the shuttle from the ship into town and were actually on our own. After a walk around a few of the sights, we sat outside a bar, enjoying a cool drink. And what had we talked about? Nothing I could remember. What I do remember was sitting there, people-watching as Pete found the wifi code and got busy checking his phone. He'd mumbled on about some player his football club were trying to buy. It hurt but the truth was, we were already a *couple like this.*

Was it too late? Would he change now? I've still got hopes and dreams and I so want them to be with him.

It was a week later and one of the last days of the cruise when I was hurt again; the reason I ended up crying on my bed alone in our stateroom.

Pete and I had just had a lovely lunch in the restaurant and I was in a very relaxed and happy frame of mind. Over a week had passed since that afternoon conversation with Jane. I'd since pulled myself together and decided to put all those thoughts away until we were home. They hadn't gone away, though. Anything but. However, I was determined to enjoy the rest of the holiday, come what may. I parked all my frustrations and let Pete enjoy doing what Pete wanted, without question or comment.

Accepting that that would mean not being together for long periods meant I'd actually ended up having an enjoyable time. Relaxing by the pool, line dance classes, a massage and swimming had all gone down a treat.

As we were leaving the restaurant, I caught sight of the couple I'd been watching dance since the start of the cruise. I guessed they were about our age, the lady slightly older maybe, but they looked so happy together. Not only did they dance superbly but they were always chatting to one another as well as to other couples they'd met in the dancing circle. In a nutshell, they were everything I wanted for Pete and myself. I actually found myself hating them but realised this was just jealousy. I should have been pleased for them but my own situation with Pete only fed the envy and anger that bubbled away inside me.

Maybe in my head I planned for a potential conversation with them, only I never knew if the situation would present itself or how I'd feel at the time.

Now they were walking past, hand in hand and looking relaxed, so I suddenly seized the moment. I thought Pete would stop alongside me but he seemed to wander on and stop just out of earshot. Typical, I thought.

'Hello. I just had to say how much I've loved watching you both dance. It's made my holiday so enjoyable. You're so good.'

'Thank you very much,' the lady replied with a warm smile. 'That's really nice of you to say. My husband and I just love dancing and the music has been great for our style of dance. I'm so glad you enjoyed watching.'

'I've seen you up a few times.' The husband joined in the chat now and I was flattered he'd noticed me the few times I had danced. 'If you like it, why don't you and your fella have a go at dancing?'

As he said this, he glanced over to Pete, who was now reading the daily programme he'd pulled out of his pocket. It was so embarrassing. I thought he would have at least come back over when he saw me talking.

'Er, no,' I managed to reply. 'I'm afraid my husband doesn't dance.' I was annoyed the conversation had drifted to this, possibly the one thing I didn't want to talk about.

'I was wondering if I could ask you a favour,' I went on quickly. 'I see you mainly dance modern jive. I had a lesson last year and loved it. I wondered if I could borrow your husband for a dance later.'

I directed the question to the wife as I thought this would be the most polite way of asking. I also thought it was a harmless enough request and in my mind, I was already looking forward to a dance later with this guy I'd watched and admired all holiday.

What I was completely unprepared for was her reply.

'I'm sorry, no. Please don't be offended but we're on holiday. It's our time together and I want to dance with my husband. I always have to share him at home and this is where I get him to myself.'

With that, she made a point of squeezing his hand as if to emphasise, *'He's mine'*.

Ouch! To say I was shocked was an understatement. In the space of a few seconds I'd gone from relaxed and happy to dumbfounded. Had I just heard that right? I'd stopped to praise them and she'd said that. I already wanted the ground to open up and swallow me when her husband almost apologetically joined in.

'We actually help out a lot on the dance scene back home, so my wife goes whole nights without dancing with me. Hey, you must get your guy dancing. Once you get the bug it's a life-changer. Ladies love their guys to dance, right? It'll open up a whole new social life for you both.'

This just added insult to injury. If only he knew how much I wanted to get *'my guy'* dancing. Of course I wanted a new social life. Was he doing this on purpose knowing Pete was lurking just out of earshot? Probably. I'd heard enough and, with a forced smile, I made my exit.

I could hardly look at Pete as he joined me on the walk back to the cabin. He dared to ask about the conversation but I cut him short. Would I have wanted Pete to comfort me back in the cabin? What would he have said? Would he put his arms around me? Say he'd been selfish and of course we could start dance lessons again when we got home? It had gone way beyond that by then and, frankly, I was pleased when he said he was off to take part in a shuffleboard game on deck.

'Frank'll be there. Why don't you come along? I expect Jane'll be with him so you girls can find something to do.'

I sent him off, feigning a headache, but in truth I just wanted to be alone and sulk. That exchange had really hurt me.

As I slumped down on the bed and cried, I vowed something would change when we got home. I had no idea what but I'd think of something.

They say you look back on a turning point – and this was that time.

***

Life returned to the normal routine after the cruise and within a few weeks it was just a memory.

But there was a new spring in my step because I had a goal. The trouble was I had no idea at that point what it was. During the coffee mornings with Pat I still found myself talking about Pete but by then, it had turned more into a resignation of how things were rather than the plans I had to change him so he'd spend more quality time with me. I talked about the cruise but only about the places, the lovely food and the shows. Again, because of Pat being widowed, I left out the events that had caused problems with Pete. But the hurt was still there and it hit me again in one of our conversations.

One morning, we'd been reminiscing about a trip we'd all been on many years ago when her husband was still alive. They'd not had their son then, so it was just the three of them, Pete, me and the girls. We'd had a lovely afternoon walk after a pub lunch. Pat was remembering with fondness when we'd come across a wishing well.

'Do you remember, Shirley? We all threw in a coin, even the children. I never did get my wish. What about you?'

My mind had already gone back to that day as Pat asked the question. In view of her circumstances I was reserved with my reply.

'Do you know, I can't remember, Pat. It was a lovely day but that bit escapes me.'

With that, I moved the conversation on and another session ended.

But I remembered all right. As if it was yesterday.

Of course it had been pleasant to be away for that break but on the day in question, I was thirty-four years old going on eighty. I felt like an old lady with the stresses of two teenage daughters, trying to juggle my hairdressing course and be a wife. Pete was working hard, of course, but even then I felt I was doing it all and not getting any encouragement or support.

As I threw a twenty pence coin into the well, I made my wish. As clear as day, I can see the coin falling.

'I just want to be happy.'

***

It was late August and I'd been on a shopping trip with Amy and Caroline. As it transpired, I was so pleased I'd gone that day. Pete found it hard to sound disappointed when the girls asked me over breakfast if I wanted to join them. I checked with him in case he had something up his sleeve he was waiting to surprise me with. For all I knew, he could have had a romantic day planned… Not!

'Thanks, girls, that'd be lovely if you don't mind having your old mum in tow,' I said. 'Pete, had you anything planned for today?'

'No, love, you go ahead and have a lovely day,' he replied. 'I've got some jobs to be getting on with.'

That's the romantic day out of the window, then, I thought. As if. As for the jobs, that would be something to do with the pub or football.

Then I remembered hearing on the news the night before that his team were away in London and he'd not mentioned travelling. Did I care? It did, however, cross my mind why he hadn't thought to take me on a weekend away to London. I would have been happy to take in the game if it meant a night in a swanky hotel, a meal and a show. I struggled to remember the last time we'd been to a show together. There were shows on the cruise, of course, but that was different. And I'd been to see the *Strictly Tour Show* with the girls at the start of the year, but would he come? Apparently it had clashed with a midweek game so that had been right out of the question. Even then, he couldn't leave it there and had a childish dig at Caroline's boyfriend, who ended up the only man in our group, which included Pat and some other friends of the girls.

I'd really enjoyed that night and remember how the women in the audience had so outnumbered the men. I'd taken a long look around the arena and, with Pete in mind along with my frustrations from the September before still festering, I thought, What is it that men don't get about us women loving dance?

Anyway, what was I thinking? No chance that weekend so a shopping trip it was.

Why was I still clutching at straws? For a while there I'd been willing to go to football, even to try to get to like it if it meant we could be together. Stay strong, I thought, a plan will come to me.

The shopping trip was a bit of a rollercoaster of emotions for me. For the first part of the day, I felt my age as the girls dragged me around fashion shops. We visited a large retail complex half an hour's drive away and their choice of shops did nothing for me. Amy worked in one of the shops so was eager to show Caroline a new range that had come in for the winter. They wanted designer labels; I was more at home in the local charity shops. How they'd ridiculed me for that through the years. Like any couple with a young family, the early years had been spent scrimping and saving so we could provide for the girls and I'd just got into the habit of looking for a bargain. This had stuck with me. Even on our cruise at least three of my evening dresses were from charity shops.

I had money now, of course, but it didn't even occur to me that day to look for anything. So for the best part of the morning, I was happy to do the mum thing and they were soon carrying bags of new clothes.

Dinner followed, on me, of course. I had no reason at that point to think anything would change in the afternoon and shopping-wise I was right. But then something did happen. Something that turned on a lightbulb in my head. Thinking back, this was the fateful moment.

'Hi there, how are you?' a voice said. 'Long time, no see. My God, it must have been your party.'

I recognised the couple. More to the point, I recognised the man. I'd met him last November at Caroline's engagement party. I'd really enjoyed that night. In fact, it was the last time I can honestly remember feeling so good.

It was Dave's, Caroline's fiancé's, older sister and her husband we bumped into that day. They'd spotted Caroline and woven through the shoppers to speak. It didn't take me long to remember the man's name – James – and that night at the party, he'd asked me to dance.

Being a special night, we'd taken a taxi and, for once, I'd allowed myself a few glasses of wine. This had loosened me up a bit and I'd enjoyed joining in the fun, which included a good deal of dancing. James and his wife had been dancing modern jive and I remember Amy telling them I'd been to lessons. A slight exaggeration but he asked me to dance and, for the third time in those few months, I loved every minute of it.

After some general catching up, James turned to me.

'So, it's lovely to see you again. How's the dancing going?'

'It's great to see you both too,' I replied. 'I think Amy might have been telling a porky that night. I'd only been to the one lesson with Pete but I'm afraid it wasn't for him and that was it.'

Still smarting from the experience on the cruise, I was very careful to address both of them. For all I knew, Dave's sister might have taken a dislike to me so I was quite happy to dismiss the whole thing. James, however, wasn't phased.

'What? That's outrageous. You're a natural.' He turned to Caroline and Amy. 'Your mum's a great dancer. Tell her she needs to persuade your dad. What's she thinking of? Mind you, that would explain something.'

'James, don't go there.' Dave's sister suddenly jumped in. 'Leave that alone now, it's nearly a year ago.'

I was instantly intrigued. 'No, carry on. You've got me interested now. You can't just leave it there. Honestly, I don't mind and you won't upset me,' I lied.

James took a look at his wife, who was still frowning a little but seemed to accept he'd gone too far now to backtrack.

'Well, it was probably nothing and I stress it's all water under the bridge now but, I was a bit upset that night. It was either that your husband wasn't pleased I'd danced with you or perhaps the drink. Maybe both but he came over a bit annoyed.'

I noticed Dave's sister was nodding her head in agreement now.

'So, what did he say?' I enquired.

'It's not what he said,' James continued. 'He just acted a bit of a prat, if I'm honest. I'm sorry. I know he's your husband and Caroline's dad.'

James's wife could see he was feeling awkward and jumped in.

'Basically, what James is trying to say is that he came onto the dance floor near the end of the evening and tried to deliberately bump into us. It's lucky James had his wits about him and got me off the floor before your husband had his way, but I wouldn't have been amused if I'd been hurt. James loved having a dance with you that night and I was happy for you both, but that was out of order. Still,' she finished, 'as James says, it's all water under the bridge now so let's not dwell on it anymore.'

The girls then quickly turned the conversation round and it was forgotten.

At the end, as they were leaving, I noticed James give me an extra-long glance and smile. I returned the smile with interest, being careful his wife didn't notice as she was busy kissing Caroline goodbye. It was just a glance, but one that aroused a flicker inside me. I was also seething with anger at what James and his wife had told me about Pete. I'd missed it at the party but I had seen this stupid, jealous behaviour on the cruise ship.

I needed to get home then but, boy, was I glad of that meeting. It both aroused my passion for dancing and banged another nail into the coffin of my rapidly fading marriage. On the way home that day, I heard on the radio that Pete's team had won three-nil and this just added to the irritation I felt towards him.

We got back early in the evening, just in time for a quick bite to eat before the three of us settled down to watch Strictly. But as I watched and loved the dancing, that evening my mind was distracted by something very real. Pete was out, as was to be expected, and I wasn't worried what time he intended rolling in that night.

Later on, I poured a glass of wine to celebrate. I had a plan at last. I just needed to make that plan a reality. That was the test. I had hopes and dreams and the time to start was right now. The experiment must begin.

Leaning forward, I picked up the phone and called my trusted friend, Pat.

'Hi Pat, it's Shirley.' I paused; took a deep breath. 'How do you fancy us two going dancing next Thursday? No partner needed it says on the leaflet. I really want to do this. Will you come with me? Let's have some fun!'

About the Author

Enjoying over twenty years in and around the social dance scene, A K Hazelton decided to create a fictional story based on their experiences. Witnessing how the behavioural traits of people in the dancing world manifested into everyday life, this became a golden opportunity to bring these to life with a book about a 'happily married couple!'

'The Wife who Wanted to Dance' is their first book and they're busy writing the follow up!